Girl Meets Boy

DEREK STRANGE

Level I

Series Editor: Derek Strange

PENGUIN BOOKS

PENGUIN BOOKS

Published by the Penguin Group
Penguin Books Ltd, 27 Wrights Lane, London W8 5TZ, England
Penguin Books USA Inc., 375 Hudson Street, New York, New York 10014, USA
Penguin Books Australia Ltd, Ringwood, Victoria, Australia
Penguin Books Canada Ltd, 10 Alcorn Avenue, Toronto, Ontario, Canada M4V 3B2
Penguin Books (NZ) Ltd, 182-190 Wairau Road, Auckland 10, New Zealand

Penguin Books Ltd, Registered Offices: Harmondsworth, Middlesex, England

First published by Penguin Books 1995
1 3 5 7 9 10 8 6 4 2

Text copyright © Derek Strange 1995
Illustrations copyright © Bob Harvey (Pennant Illustration Agency) 1995
All rights reserved

The moral right of the author and of the illustrator has been asserted

Illustrations by Bob Harvey (Pennant Illustration Agency)

Printed in England by Clays Ltd, St Ives Plc
Set in 12/14 pt Lasercomp Bembo by Datix International Limited, Bungay, Sufolk

Girl Meets Boy

And suddenly there he was, this tall, quiet boy in a blue and white shirt . . . I'll always remember the first time I saw him.

Donna is on a boat. She is going to Spain with her family for a holiday. On the boat she sees Mark, a tall, good-looking boy. But Mark is very shy and he doesn't talk to her on the boat. Who will help them to meet? Will they be together?

Derek Strange writes books and stories for young people. He lives in London with his family. He has one son; his name is Mark. In July 1993, Derek and Mark went to Spain on a boat for a holiday . . .

To the teacher:

The main verb forms and tenses used at Level One are:

- *be* and *have*, *there is* and *there are*, imperatives, the present simple tense of regular verbs and irregular forms of listed verbs, present continuous verbs with present time meaning, present continuous verbs with future time meaning and the past simple tense of regular verbs
- modal verbs: *can* (to express ability, permission and possibility) and *will* (to talk about the future).

Also used are:

- adverbs: of frequency, place, time and manner (regular forms only)
- prepositions: of place and time
- adjectives: of shape, size and colour, demonstrative, possessive and interrogative adjectives
- conjunctions: *and*, *but* and *or*.

Specific attention is paid to vocabulary development in the Vocabulary Work exercises at the end of the book. These exercises are aimed at training students to enlarge their vocabulary systematically through intelligent reading and effective use of a dictionary

To the student:

Dictionary Words:

- Some words in this book are dark black. Find them in your dictionary or try to understand them with no dictionary first.

Donna's story

My story starts in late July. It was July 21st, I think. It was the first day of our holiday, a hot July day. I stood in the sun and looked at the sea. It was eleven o'clock in the morning. I was on the boat at Portsmouth with my mother and father and my sister, Louise. Sea **birds** played near our big boat and the small boats near us on the sea.

I started to look at the people with us on our boat. They all watched the sea birds and talked and **laughed**. They were all happy on the first day of their holiday too. And suddenly there he was, this tall, quiet boy in a blue and white shirt: he was *really* **good-looking**. I'll always remember the first time I saw him.

Wow! He's lovely.

Look!

He didn't see me then. He was with some friends.
One of the boys was his brother, I think: they had the
same blue eyes, the same mouth and nose, nearly the
same hair. His brother and one of the boys with him
tried to catch the sea birds and he smiled at them. Then
they came and stood near us, and they talked about the
small boats on the sea. I watched him over Louise's
head all the time!

His brother and his friends made a lot of noise, but he was quiet and didn't talk a lot. Then suddenly he looked at me and his eyes stayed quietly on me . . . and he smiled his lovely smile with his **shy** blue eyes.

The people near me on the boat, the sun, the sea, the birds, the noise of his friends, time – it all stopped. At that **moment** there was only him and me, me and him. Him and his smile for me. Only the two of us.

Slowly, very slowly, the boat started to move away, across the water to Spain. It takes a day and a night on the boat from Portsmouth to Santander, in Spain. A day and a night **together**, on the same boat with him . . .

We'll be on this boat for a day and a night. Perhaps I can talk to him before we arrive there . . . Perhaps I'll see him again this evening . . .

It was a big new boat with cafes, shops, a cinema and a **disco**. In the evening Louise and I went to the disco together. We had a Coke and listened to the **music** and watched the **dancers**. But he wasn't there.

Then suddenly a tall boy in a black and white shirt came in – it was him! He was with a friend. They stopped and looked slowly at all the people in the disco. It was dark in there and he stood and looked for a long time.

Then he saw me and he smiled a big, friendly smile. I wanted to stand up and sing and dance . . . dance with *him*. He came across the room and stopped near our table . . . and he asked me to dance!

Suddenly he wasn't shy with me. We danced together for a long time after that.

But then I looked up and there was a second tall boy in a blue and white shirt at the door of the disco, with the same eyes and the same mouth and nearly the same hair.

But the boy near the door had that **nice**, quiet, shy face – not a big, open, friendly smile. Suddenly I knew: this was his brother with me on the dance-floor, not *him*! I was with the wrong brother!

He stood for a moment near the door and watched me and his brother on the dance-floor with sad eyes. I wanted to run to him, to take his sad face in my hands and say 'sorry'. He looked at me, then he went out quickly.

I stopped dancing, walked back to my table and sat down. His brother started to dance with Louise.

I didn't sleep that night. I thought about him all the time, and listened to the noises of the boat and the sea. In the morning I went to the café at eight o'clock and waited there with my sister for a long time. I wanted to say 'sorry' to him. I had four cups of coffee, and I don't really like coffee.

But he didn't come. Where was he? Where was he?

At eleven o'clock we arrived in Santander. I wanted to stop the boat: I wanted to stop the holiday; I wanted to go back to England. I only wanted to see him again, to talk to him, to ask his name.

But he wasn't there.

Where are you?
I want to see you again.

Mark's story

I started Spanish at school in September and I like it.
We've got a good teacher – Old Webb. '*Mr* Webb,
not *Old* Webb,' my mother always says to me.
'He isn't old, you know.'

Old Webb – sorry, *Mr* Webb - always
takes some people from our school to a
place in Spain for the first two weeks of
the holidays, every July. Old Webb is
OK. Not bad, for a teacher.

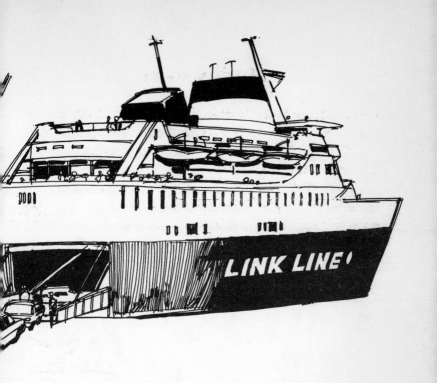

We were at Portsmouth with Old Webb – sorry, *Mr* Webb – and Mrs Webb. She's from Argentina; all the boys think she's good-looking, too. There were six of us with the Webbs: Harry Potts and his sister Sonia, Nick Atkins (he's a good friend), Sue Bellamy (she's clever), my brother Dave and me (we're fourteen and we're good friends too . . . usually).

There were hundreds of people on the boat. It was hot in the sun, a lovely day. People watched the sea and the small boats. I liked being in the sun and thinking about the two weeks holiday in Spain. Old Webb started one of his stories about Argentina, but I didn't listen. I started to look at the people. And this girl was there, near me, a really good-looking girl with nice brown eyes and black hair.

I'm really shy and I'm not very good with girls. I didn't talk to her then, but I watched her with her sister and her mother and father. Then they walked away and she smiled at me for a moment before they went. My brother Dave saw her, and he laughed quietly at my red face.

> Hey! She's smiling at you . . . and you're all red in the face – you're in love! Hey, man! You're in love!

I wanted to see her again, perhaps in the café at lunch-time, or perhaps in the cinema in the afternoon. But she wasn't there and I don't remember the film.

In the evening we had a drink with Old Webb and Lovely Lucrezia (that's our name for Mrs Webb). After that Dave and Harry went to the disco – they wanted to meet some girls. I don't like dancing, but I went to the disco later: I wanted to see *her* again, the lovely girl with the dancing brown eyes and the nice smile.

It was dark in the disco, and I stood near the door and watched the dancers. Then I saw her on the dance-floor . . . and she was with Dave! With my brother, Dave! She smiled at him, too, a lovely smile.

I didn't want to watch; I walked out. I went and looked at the sea and thought about things quietly. I thought about her, her and Dave.

I was up early in the morning, before six o'clock. I went out again and watched the early morning sun and the sea. There was only one old man and the sea birds there with me. The old man smiled at me, but we didn't talk. I liked being quiet.

I went in and had a coffee in the café, but I didn't want to eat. All the time I wanted to see *her*. I wanted her to walk into the café and come across to my table and sit down with me and tell me her name and talk to me. But she didn't come. I waited and waited, but she didn't come.

At eight o'clock I went to find Nick and Dave. Dave was very quiet all day, and he was really nice to me. And I didn't see *her* again before we arrived in Santander at eleven.

She wasn't there.

Will she come?

The town's story

Comillas is a small town fifty kilometres from Santander, near the sea. In the town there are quiet streets of old buildings and there is a small **square**. There are small shops and cafés with tables and chairs in the square, under the trees. A lot of people from Madrid come to Comillas for their holidays, and a lot of people from England stay in the town too. In the evenings in June and July and August people like to walk in the streets of Comillas. They stop in the square and stand and talk together; their children play together. Some people sit at the café tables and have a drink and watch the children or read their newspapers or talk.

It was disco-night in Comillas on the evening after the boat arrived in Santander from Portsmouth. There were a lot of people in the square – Spanish people from Comillas and Madrid, but families from England and France and Germany and Holland too. Some of the English families from the boat were there now, in Comillas for a night or two.

Donna was there with her family, at a table under some trees. Her eyes were on the dancers . . . but she didn't see them; the music was in her ears . . . but she didn't hear it. She didn't want to look or listen or dance; she didn't want to *be* there. She only wanted to see the lovely, shy boy from the boat, perhaps to dance with him.

First Mr and Mrs Webb wanted to go to a little place near the beach where they always had good fish. They wanted to have a good time on their first evening in Spain, and later there was the disco in the square at Comillas . . .

Let's go and eat at one of the places down near the beach. Then we can go to the disco in the square at Comillas. OK?

Yeah! Right!

Mark didn't want to go. He didn't want to eat or dance or talk and laugh. He wanted to sit quietly and think about the good-looking girl on the boat. Where was she now? But Dave and Harry and Nick and Sue all wanted him to go . . .

Later that evening he walked into the square at Comillas with his friends. They found a table at one of the cafés and they all sat down.

Mark looked slowly at the people at the tables near them . . . Donna looked sadly at the people dancing and standing in the square . . . then their eyes met.

Time stopped. He was *here!* She was *here!*

He smiled at her with his nice blue eyes. She smiled back at him with her dark brown eyes. Suddenly he wasn't shy. He stood up and started to walk across to her . . . she was on her feet. Their hands met. She wanted to dance now, only with him!

The others watched and smiled – they all knew. And Dave? Dave watched and smiled happily. You see, only Dave *really* knew the story. Only Dave knew his plan for his brother.

And Donna and Mark started to dance. They were together.

Exercises

Vocabulary Work

Look again at the 'Dictionary Words' in this story. Are they nouns or verbs or adjectives? Write the words and write N (for noun), V (for verb) or A (for adjective), e.g. story (N), bird (N).
Then write short sentences with the new words.

Comprehension

Answer the questions.

Donna's story
1   (page 5) When was the first day of Donna's holiday?
2   (page 6) Where was she when she first saw Mark?
3   (page 9) How long were Donna and Mark on the boat together?
4   (page 12) Who was on the dance-floor with Donna when she saw Mark at the door of the disco?
5   (page 15) At what time did the boat arrive in Santander?

Mark's story
6   (page 16) What is Mark's name for his Spanish teacher?
7   page 16) How long was Mark's holiday in Spain?
8   (page 22) What did Mark do when he got up early in the morning?

The town's story
9   (page 24) Where is Comillas?
10 (page 24) What do people do in the square in Comillas in the evenings in July and August?
11 (page 26) Who wanted Mark to go to the dance in Comillas?
12 (page 30) What *was* Dave's plan for Mark?

Discussion

1   Are you shy? When and why (or why not)?
2   Do you like dancing and discos? Why or why not?

3   What music do you like for dancing? And for listening to quietly?

Writing

1   You are Dave. Write a short letter from Comillas to a friend
     back in England (80 words). Tell her/him about Donna and
     Mark on the boat.
2   Write 100 words about one of *your* holidays. Where were you?
     Who was with you? What did you do on the first day or two?
     Did you make new friends?